The Scariest Stories You've Ever Heard,
PART II

The Scariest Stories You've Ever Heard,

PART II

by Katherine Burt

To the spinners of tall tales in my family,
who are the best storytellers

Cover illustration by Richard Kriegler

Published by Willowisp Press
801 94th Avenue North, St. Petersburg, Florida 33702

Copyright © 1989 by Willowisp Press,
a division of PAGES, Inc.

Printed in the United States of America

8 10 9

ISBN 0-87406-419-8

Contents

The Doctor's Visitor

A cold wind blew dead leaves past his office window as Dr. Watkins looked out at the darkening October sky. *We're in for a pretty wild storm,* he thought. The doctor heard the bell ringing in the church tower across the street. It was 10:00. *It's late,* he thought. *I'm glad I'll be home soon.*

He watched the moon rise through the bare branches of the old oak tree. Something about the cold whiteness of the moon against the black sky made him shiver.

Dr. Watkins had just turned back to the large stack of papers and reports on his desk when he heard a knock at the door of his office.

Who on earth would be out on a night like this? he wondered.

Opening the door, the doctor was surprised to find an old woman standing there. She was so pale and thin that the doctor thought she must be very sick. "Come in. Come in," he said in a kindly tone. "You shouldn't be out on a night like this. And you aren't even wearing a coat," he said.

"Doctor, there's a sick boy who needs your help right now," the pale woman said. She thrust a folded sheet of paper into the doctor's hand. "Please go to this address at once. There's no time to lose."

The doctor looked at the old piece of paper with its old-fashioned handwriting and saw that the address was a few miles out of town. He heard fat raindrops starting to splatter against the window pane. A bolt of lightning lighted up the dark sky, followed by a clap of thunder that seemed to echo down the streets of the village. The doctor thought of the warm fire that would be blazing at home, and the cup of tea his wife would fix for him.

But then he looked at the pale, thin old woman standing in his office. He saw the pleading in her strangely bright eyes. He read again the address on the musty old piece of paper she had given him. He noticed the faded flowery decorations on the edge of the paper and wondered where the woman could have gotten such an old kind of writing paper. He set the piece of paper on his desk.

With a sigh, Dr. Watkins said, "I usually don't make house calls this late. Don't you think you could take the child to the clinic tomorrow morning?"

The woman's eyes seemed to become even brighter with a strange fire in them. "I couldn't take the boy anywhere," the woman answered. "And what kind of doctor are you that you will not go to a dying child?" she added angrily.

"Dying? Why didn't you say so? What's wrong with the boy?" the doctor asked as he opened the closet to get his coat and medical bag. "And how do you know he's dying?" he asked as he pulled on his overcoat.

As Dr. Watkins turned to hear her answer, he noticed again how very thin the pale woman was. The white skin on her face seemed stretched so tightly that her cheekbones jutted out. Her hair was white and wispy. Her hands looked like they were made of fine china. Only her bright eyes seemed alive. They blazed with a strange fire.

Even the clothes she wore were rumpled and somehow different. Her dress looked formal, almost like an old-fashioned wedding dress.

"You ask me how I know the boy is dying, doctor," she said almost in a whisper. "Believe me, I know what a dying person looks like. You must hurry. There is no time to lose."

"I'll lock up, and we'll go right away. Wait for me here."

"Oh, doctor," the woman said quietly. "Thank you for going to the boy. Thank you."

"I am a doctor," he answered. "And doctors go to sick people."

The woman had a strange little half-smile on her pale face. Then she said, "Yes, doctors go to sick people."

Something in the woman's tone and strange half-smile made him feel uneasy. "Uh, please wait here. I'll be right back after I lock up." The doctor hurried down the hall.

"You can ride over with..." he started to say as he walked back into the waiting room. But the room was empty. The old woman was gone. "I'm ready to leave now," he called out. But only the silence answered.

He searched all the rooms of his office. But the pale old woman was not there. Had he dreamed the whole visit? Maybe he had been working too hard lately. Here he was, still at the office at 10:00 at night. And the woman did seem a little strange.

But then Dr. Watkins saw the handwritten note with the address on his desk. He picked it up and read the address again. And below the house number were written the words,

"Doctors go to sick people."

So, he hadn't dreamed it. The old woman had been there.

"Well," said the doctor out loud, "I guess I'd better go on out there."

He turned out the lights in his office. In the darkness, he noticed once again the strange musty smell of the woman's clothes. A bolt of lightning lighted up the sky as he closed the door to his office. Dr. Watkins pulled his coat tightly around him and walked to his car.

He drove through the worsening storm. The thunder and lightning seemed to explode every few seconds, and the rain smacked against his windshield. It took him 15 minutes to reach the house, an old farmhouse off by itself on the edge of a woods.

He looked at the old woman's note to check the address. When he saw it was the right house, he folded the note up and put it back in his pocket. When he knocked on the big front door, the doctor was greeted by a man in his thirties.

"May I help you?" the man asked with a puzzled look on his face.

"I'm Dr. Watkins. I'm here for the sick child," he answered.

The man looked at the doctor's medical bag

and then asked, "What sick child? Our son Timothy is upstairs asleep. He's not sick. I don't understand."

A young woman appeared at the door behind the man.

"Who is it, Jack?" she asked.

"It's a doctor who says he's here about a sick child."

"Look, I was told by an old woman to come to this address because a boy was dying," Dr. Watkins explained. "May I come in? I'm getting soaked standing here."

"Yes, of course," the young woman said, opening the door wide. "Come in, and tell us what's going on."

Sitting in the living room, the doctor told them about the strange, pale visitor. "The old woman insisted that I come immediately. She kept saying that there was no time to lose. Now I get here, and I find that nobody is..."

Here the doctor suddenly stopped talking. His eyes fell on a framed photograph on a desk in the corner of the living room.

"That woman there, in the photograph," he said, pointing toward the desk. "That's her! That's the woman who was in my office!"

The couple looked at each other for a moment. Then the woman said, "You must be mistaken, doctor. That's my mother. She's been dead for over three years."

"But she gave me this address," he answered, handing her the folded up piece of paper.

The young woman opened the old piece of paper, looking at her husband. When she saw what was written on it, she gasped. "It can't be! It can't be true!" she screamed.

"What is it?" both men cried.

"It's a page from my mother's prayer book. I put it in her coffin right before she was buried," the woman said in a hoarse whisper.

Then she looked up toward their son's bedroom with wild eyes. "She must know!" she screamed. "Mother knows!"

The woman flew up the stairs, with the note in her hand. The men were right behind her. They found Timothy unconscious on his bed.

Dr. Watkins felt the boy's forehead and announced, "He's burning up with fever. It might be meningitis. Call an ambulance! If we get him to the hospital right away, we can save him."

The young woman had collapsed on her son's bed. Dr. Watkins took the note from her hand and showed it to Jack.

"But what does it mean? Why did she write 'Doctors go to sick people'?" Dr. Watkins asked.

Jack stared at the old-fashioned handwriting on the old musty prayer book page. He swallowed hard and then said, "Doctor, my wife's mother died right here, in this room, of a heart attack. We called a doctor, and we waited almost five hours. By the time he got here, she was dead."

Brenda's New Dress

BRENDA had always wanted to be like the other girls in the senior class. She had always wanted to be invited to dances and parties. But there was something different about her, something she couldn't change.

Brenda had lived with her mother since her parents' divorce, and there just wasn't very much money. She had never been able to afford the clothes and nice things that the other girls had. Brenda just didn't fit in with the popular crowd.

That's why she was so excited when Jason asked her to the big spring dance. Brenda had liked Jason for a long time. He didn't seem to mind that her clothes looked like they came from the Salvation Army. Brenda's mom always made sure that her clothes were clean and mended. They just weren't the latest styles from the expensive stores at the mall.

But Brenda couldn't wear her old clothes to the dance. She had to find some way to get a beautiful formal dress.

Brenda pleaded with her mother to let her get a dress. "Please, Mom," Brenda said that night at dinner. "All the other kids will have fancy dresses. Can't we find the money somewhere? Jason is one of the neatest guys in the whole school."

Her mother sighed. "I know how much this means to you, Brenda," she explained. "But there just isn't any extra money for things like a formal dress."

Brenda tried to keep the tears from her eyes. She knew how hard things were for her mother. But she wanted to go to the dance so badly.

That weekend they went to several rental companies to look at formal dresses for the dance. Brenda couldn't believe how much they were asking, just to rent the dresses. The dance was only a week away. She was going to have to tell Jason that she couldn't go with him.

Then her mother said, "I know one more place we can try. There's a pawnshop on the west side. Let's give it a try. It's got to be cheaper than these places."

The pawnshop was on a small side street

in an old, dark building. And there in the shop, hanging next to a black suit, was a beautiful blue satin evening gown. It had a white lace collar, and it looked like it had hardly been worn at all.

"Oh, Mom!" cried Brenda. "I love it! It's perfect!"

Brenda held the blue dress up to her in front of a mirror. It seemed to be her size.

"I feel like someone in a fairy tale!" she exclaimed to her smiling mother. "I feel like I'm Cinderella or Sleeping Beauty."

The only problem was the dress' odd smell. It didn't smell bad, just strange. It reminded Brenda of something, but she couldn't quite place it. The smell of the dress brought back a picture in Brenda's mind of her grandmother. And Brenda hadn't seen her grandmother since she died 12 years ago.

"We can air it out for a few days," her mother said. "That should take care of that smell."

Walking out of the pawnshop after buying the dress, Brenda loved how the deep blue of the beautiful dress shone in the sun. "Mom," she said, "I just know this dance is going to be one of the best nights in my whole life."

The night of the big dance finally arrived.

Brenda looked beautiful in the blue gown. She had put on a little more perfume than usual because the dress still had a faint smell. You could hardly notice it anymore, though—the perfume and airing it out took care of it.

The school gymnasium was packed, and everyone there commented what a great-looking couple Jason and Brenda were. They danced almost every dance together.

But as they were dancing, Brenda noticed she was feeling a little dizzy.

"Jason, do you mind if we sit down for a while?" she asked. "I'm feeling kind of weak. I'm sure I'll feel better in a minute."

When Jason came back with a drink of water for her, Brenda was feeling a lot worse. "I guess I danced so much that I made myself sick," she said. "I'm really sorry, Jason. I've had the best time of my life. But could you take me home early?"

When Brenda got home, she was even more tired and dizzy than she had been at the dance. When she caught a glimpse of herself in the hall mirror, she noticed that her skin had turned a pale white. *It's nothing a little sleep won't cure,* she thought.

Brenda kissed her mother good night and climbed slowly upstairs to her bedroom. She couldn't wait to lay her head down on her pillow. Without even changing out of her blue dress, Brenda lay down on her bed and fell into a deep sleep.

When Brenda didn't come downstairs the next morning for breakfast, her mother was a little worried. "Brenda," she called up the stairs. But there was no answer. Then her mother knocked on Brenda's door. There was still no answer.

"Come on, get up, you sleepyhead," her mother said, opening the door. But she wasn't prepared for what she found inside.

There was Brenda, lying very still, in her blue gown spread out around her on her bed. Her face, which had been so pale the night before, had turned greenish.

With a cry, Brenda's mother reached out to shake her awake, but Brenda's skin was cold and clammy. She couldn't wake her up.

It was then that Brenda's mother noticed the odor, that strange sweet odor that they had smelled when they purchased the dress at the pawnshop. It was the odor that Brenda had tried to disguise with perfume the night before. Suddenly, she thought she knew what the smell was. It smelled almost like...

"NO!" screamed Brenda's mother as she ran down the stairs to call the ambulance.

When the ambulance and doctor arrived,

the emergency team ran up the stairs to Brenda's room. After a few minutes, the doctor came out of Brenda's room to speak to her mother. The doctor shook his head.

"I'm very sorry," he said sadly. "There was nothing we could do to save your daughter. I've never seen a case like this in my 30 years as a doctor."

The doctor took off his glasses. "You see," he explained. "Your daughter has in her blood an extremely high concentration of a chemical that stopped her blood from flowing. We have no idea how she could have gotten such a massive dose of the chemical."

Brenda's mother felt faint and leaned against the wall to keep from falling. "What is the chemical, doctor?" she asked in a whisper.

The doctor paused. "We're not sure," he said. "But we believe it's embalming fluid."

"No! No!" wailed Brenda's mother hysterically as she burst into the bedroom and collapsed on her daughter's lifeless body. She cried until the emergency team gently led her away.

Later that day, a police car pulled up in front of the old, dark pawnshop where Brenda's mother had purchased the blue gown. The doctor and a policeman were taking a statement from the manager.

"Yes," explained the confused manager, "I remember the dress. It was in a big pile of clothing that one of my assistants took in. He no longer works here, but I think I can find the receipt from that bunch of clothes."

The manager put on his glasses and began to search through a large box with many receipts and sales forms.

"Ah, yes," he said, holding up a piece of paper. "Here it is—a blue evening gown."

The doctor and policeman leaned closer.

"Oh, dear," said the manager.

"What is it?" asked the doctor anxiously.

"That blue dress was sold to my assistant by the Dodds Funeral Home, just down the street," said the manager. "They used it to dress a corpse for a funeral."

The Deadly Dare

JOSH, Robert, and Bret were sophomores in high school and best friends. They lived in the same neighborhood and did almost everything together. One of their favorite things to do was to camp out in the woods at the end of their street. They would take their sleeping bags and sleep under the stars. They loved telling each other scary stories around the campfire.

One day Josh and Robert were bragging to some of the kids at school about their latest camping trip. "Our camping trips are great," Josh said. "Of course, a lot of people might be afraid of being out there alone. You have to be a certain kind of guy to be able to stay out there in the woods overnight. Like just last weekend, we saw a wolf."

"Yeah," Robert added. "It was a huge wolf, and we got so close to it that we could have reached out and touched it."

Bret came down the hall and saw the group gathered around his two friends. Sure, he had done his share of bragging about their campouts, but this wolf story the guys were telling was a little too much. Actually, what they had seen was a runaway German shepherd. It even had a collar around its neck.

"Oh, come on, you guys. They don't need to know about all of that," Bret said. He wanted to change the subject before somebody found out they were exaggerating the truth. Then the other kids would tease them. But it was too late.

"Hey!" came the voice of Andy Seibert, a senior. "If you sophomores are so brave, why don't you stay out in the real woods?"

"What do you mean, Andy?" asked Josh.

"My older brother has a cabin up at Lake Montuak in the state forest. If you're so brave, then why don't you stay there by yourselves for a night? Since you're so friendly with wolves, you should feel right at home there. And there are bears and cougars there, too— not to mention the state prison down the road a few miles. I bet 25 dollars you won't spend a night in that cabin alone."

The three friends couldn't stand to hear the crowd of kids laughing at what Andy said. Bret could tell the kids didn't think they'd spend the night in the cabin. All Bret knew was he didn't really like the idea of all those wild animals outside the cabin, plus the state prison down the road.

Bret's heart skipped a beat when he heard Robert say, "Well, we accept. That will be a piece of cake."

"Yeah," added Josh. "Get that 25 dollars ready."

"Yeah, sure," teased Andy. "It'll be a piece of cake. Hey, I'll even drive you there myself."

Bret went along with his buddies. But he still felt uneasy. After all, he knew the difference between a German shepherd and a wolf. He wondered if Josh and Robert did.

Late Friday afternoon, Andy drove the three boys to the cabin. When they stopped at a gas station deep in the woods, the man at the pumps saw their sleeping bags in the back of the car.

"Be careful if you're going to be out in the woods this weekend," the man said. "The man on the radio's saying that a man escaped from the prison yesterday. He's armed and dangerous." Then the man lowered his voice and looked around, like he was afraid somebody might hear him.

Who could hear him? thought Bret. *We're*

all alone out here in the middle of nowhere.

"They say the escaped guy's a little crazy, too," said the gas station man in a low voice. "He killed a whole family up in the northern part of the state."

"I wonder how much Andy paid this guy to tell us that?" Robert whispered to Josh and Bret. "He's just trying to scare us."

"Yeah," answered Josh. "And he's a lousy actor, too. That whispering bit is hokey!"

They finally reached the little cabin after a long drive up a dirt road deep in the woods. They got out of the car and stretched their legs. As Andy was helping the others unload their gear, he said, "Listen, you guys. I've been thinking about what the guy at the gas station said about that escaped murderer. If you want to call the whole thing off, that's okay with me. I won't tell anybody."

Bret started to say he was willing to call it off, but Josh butted in first. "Nice try, Andy," he said. "But you're still trying to scare us into not staying here. Then you'll tell everybody at school that we chickened out."

"Yeah," added Robert. "It won't work. Just like that thing with the guy at the gas station who you told to scare us didn't work."

"What are you guys talking about?" Andy asked. "I didn't tell him to say anything. I'm just trying to help you out if there's something dangerous up here."

"Well, we don't need your help," said Robert. "Just be here tomorrow morning to pick us up. But don't come back too early. We might want to sleep late," he joked.

"And have that 25 dollars ready!" shouted Josh.

"You guys are still talking big," said Andy. "Don't say I didn't give you a chance to back out."

Bret wished his friends hadn't been such big mouths in saying no to Andy's offer to leave. But what could he do now? He couldn't back out himself, or his friends would never let him forget it.

Before getting in his car, Andy gave Josh a flare gun. "Don't let anybody in the cabin, and keep the door and windows locked," he explained. "And if you get into any trouble, just shoot off this flare. Someone's bound to see it."

The three boys watched the taillights of Andy's car disappear down the dirt road in the twilight. The sun had just set over the tops of the tall pine trees, and it was getting dark fast.

The three friends settled quickly into the cabin, stowed their gear away, and started a fire to heat some of the cans of food they had brought with them.

After they ate, they talked about what an easy bet they had made, and they began to plan how they were going to spend the 25 dollars they would win.

"We should have bet him 50 dollars!" said Robert with a laugh.

About 10:00, the fire started to die down. The boys realized that someone needed to go out and collect some firewood in the woods. "I'll go," offered Robert. "It'll only take a few minutes," he said, pulling on his coat.

"Maybe two of us should go," Bret said. "Remember what the guy at the gas station said."

"You're a chicken!" hooted Josh. "That was all an act that Andy set up. Don't tell me you believe it!"

"Well," said Bret. "I didn't say I believed it. I—uh—just think we should be careful, that's all."

"Hey, don't worry about it, Brettie. I'll go with Robert," Josh teased.

"We'll be back to tuck you in and read you a bedtime story in a few minutes. You didn't forget to pack your teddy bear, did you?" added Robert. Josh and Robert were laughing their heads off.

"Ah, knock it off, you guys," said Bret angrily. "At least take this flare gun with you." He handed the flare to Josh. The boys went out the door and vanished into the darkness around the cabin.

After they had been gone for what seemed like a long time, Bret started to get worried. He looked out the window. But he saw nothing—just the faint outlines of the tall pine trees against the pitch black sky. "Where are they?" Bret wondered out loud. "There was plenty of wood right around the cabin."

Then it struck him that Josh and Robert were trying to scare him. *That's just like them,* he thought. *They're trying to make me think something's happened to them. They think I'm a chicken.*

About 10 minutes later, Bret suddenly heard muffled screams coming from the woods. "Go ahead, you jerks," said Bret. "You can't scare me."

After another 15 minutes, Bret heard a loud pop, and the night sky lighted up. "The flare!" exclaimed Bret. "Now they're trying to get *me* to go out there."

But then he heard nothing for almost an hour. His watch said it was past 11:00. The joke, if it was a joke, had gone on too long. It wasn't funny anymore. Where were they?

Bret had decided to open the door and call to his friends, when he heard a sound outside. It was the sound of heavy footsteps thudding up toward the cabin door. There was another sound, too, like something was being dragged across the gravel in front of the cabin. It was coming closer.

Now Bret was terrified. He felt deep in his bones that this wasn't a joke. He knew something horrible had happened to his friends. He started to pile up against the cabin door everything he could find—the heavy wooden bed from the corner, the table and chairs, their backpacks. He even blew out the lantern and cowered near the still-warm fireplace in the dark. The dragging sounds got louder and louder. When he heard a heavy thud on the front porch, he thought that it was all over for him. He tried to make himself small enough to hide in the corner of the cabin. He couldn't stop shaking. He tried to scream, but no sound would come out.

And when he thought he couldn't be more afraid, he heard, from behind the pile of furniture at the cabin door, a scratching.

The prisoner's trying to get in! Bret thought in horror. Then he heard a moaning that didn't even sound human. Bret shrunk into the corner, expecting every moment to be his last, expecting the murderer to break in the door at any moment.

The scratching and moaning went on for what seemed like forever. Bret was too terrified to even look at his watch. All he could do was bury his head in his hands to keep out the horrible sound of the escaped man trying to get in and kill him, like he had killed Josh and Robert.

Bret must have fallen asleep or fainted from fear. He woke up the next morning to the sound of a horn beeping in front of the cabin. He heard nothing else—no scratching, no moaning. He stood up stiffly from his hiding spot near the fireplace and walked to the cabin window. He saw Andy sitting in his car. He was blowing his horn and calling out Bret's name. Feeling a tremendous sense of relief, Bret began furiously clearing away the furniture from the door. He never wanted to spend another night in a cabin as long as he lived.

Bret flung open the door and started to run toward Andy's car. But before Bret even stepped out on the porch, he saw why Andy had stayed in his car. There on the porch, next to the door, lay the bodies of Josh and Robert. Their heads were crushed in. And their fingers were bloody from having scratched on the door to get in.

The Doggie's Treat

AARON wasn't feeling well at school. He had stayed up so late the night before studying for his history test that he was dead tired. *Maybe if I say I'm sick, they'll let me go home. I can do a makeup test tomorrow,* he thought.

Looking in the mirror in the restroom, he decided he did look pretty sick. Aaron called his mother at her office, and the school nurse let him go home about 10:00.

Boy, I'm glad I took the car to school today, he thought as he settled weakly into the seat of the old station wagon. *I feel too lousy to walk home.*

All he could think of on the way home was collapsing in bed. But as he pulled into the driveway, he saw the garage door. It was slightly open. Aaron figured his mom must have forgotten to close it all the way when she left that morning for work.

It's a good thing Mame is there, Aaron thought. *No one would ever try to get into the house with her guarding it.*

Aaron parked in the driveway. As he unlocked the front door of the house, he noticed how quiet the house was. *I guess it's always quiet at 10:00 in the morning. I'm never here then,* Aaron decided.

As he turned the key in the lock, he didn't hear Mame running up to the door like she always did when he came home. And she always barked loudly until she recognized the voice. Suddenly, Aaron was afraid maybe she had gotten out the crack in the garage door and run away. She was hard to catch because she was so big and strong. And Aaron definitely didn't feel well enough to go running after Mame.

In the front hall, Aaron yelled, "Mame, Mame! Where are you, girl?" He heard nothing. He put his books down on a chair and headed toward the garage to pull the door shut. As Aaron walked through the dining room into the kitchen, he thought he heard something. Listening carefully, he heard it again. It was a strange, irregular rasping sound, and it was coming from the basement.

The basement door was open. *That's odd,*

thought Aaron. His mom kept her African violets down there. The basement door was always kept closed so Mame couldn't mess up the plants.

As Aaron got closer to the door, the sounds became louder. When he peeked down the stairs, he saw a shocking sight. There, on the basement floor, was Mame. She was writhing, kicking her legs wildly, and gasping for breath. She seemed to be choking!

With a cry, Aaron raced down the stairs. Kneeling at the poor dog's side, Aaron saw that there was blood on her coat and a little on the floor. He tried to pick her up, but she was just too big—83 pounds the last time Aaron weighed her.

"It's too bad you're not a Chihuahua instead of a Doberman," Aaron said.

Mame whimpered in pain when he tried to move her. She licked his hand as Aaron tried to comfort her.

He finally managed to wrap her in an old blanket. With the blanket under her, Aaron partly dragged, partly carried Mame up the stairs and out to the empty garage. He couldn't believe what he saw in the garage.

Near the open garage door was a large pool of blood. He also saw some scraps of torn cloth. "Oh, no, Mame must be bleeding!"

Aaron cried. "I've got to get her to the vet!"

Aaron opened the garage door and dragged Mame out to the car. As he ran back up the driveway to close the garage door, he could hear her pitiful wheezing for air. Bending over to lock the garage door, Aaron heard more moaning. *Poor Mame*, he thought. *That moaning sounds almost human!*

He sped to the animal hospital as fast as the old station wagon would go. At the animal hospital, Dr. Hernandez took Mame into an examining room, but wouldn't let Aaron come along.

"There's nothing you can do for Mame here, Aaron. Why don't you go home and wait. I'll call you as soon as I know how Mame is."

Aaron agreed, even though he wanted to stay with Mame. When he got home, he called his mom at work.

"But, Mom, there's blood all over the garage floor! No, I'm not exaggerating! When you get home, you'll see," he said.

"Well, all right, then. I'll be home right away, dear," she said. "You wait for me there."

After Aaron hung up the phone, he decided to go out and try to clean up the garage. He paused at the door to the garage.

"Huh?" he said out loud. "There's that sound again." He listened. It was a soft moaning and then a loud clunk. It sounded like it was coming from upstairs.

"That's kind of weird," said Aaron, confused. "I thought it was Mame who was moaning before." He decided to go upstairs to check out the strange sound. Walking through the dining room toward the stairs, he heard another clunk. This time it came from the top of the stairs. Suddenly, the phone rang. Answering the phone in the kitchen, Aaron heard an excited voice.

"Aaron, this is Dr. Hernandez. Listen to me now, and don't ask questions. Get out of the house *immediately!* Go over to the neighbor's house, and wait for the police. Do you hear me?"

"Police? But my mom will be here soon, and I'm..."

"Aaron! Do what I tell you NOW! NOW!"

"Okay, okay, I'm going," Aaron answered. Hanging up the phone, he thought, *What's wrong with Dr. Hernandez?*

Then he heard the moaning from upstairs suddenly become louder. "Boy, that sounds like a person," he muttered. Then he heard several clunks in a row, as if something heavy were falling down the stairs.

Aaron found himself walking quickly through the kitchen. *Maybe I will just wait outside,* he told himself as he almost ran through the garage. The moaning echoed in his ears. He took a last look at the pool of blood and torn cloth on the garage floor. He shivered.

He flung open the garage door and ran out into the driveway. Aaron heard Mrs. Findley, the neighbor, screaming for him just as a police car screeched to a halt in front of the house.

Aaron and Mrs. Findley watched from the corner of the driveway as the two policemen ran into the house with their guns drawn. A few moments later they heard shouts and a long, bone-chilling scream from inside the house.

They heard a scuffle in the garage, and then the policemen came out onto the driveway. With them was a pale, wild-looking man in ripped, dark clothes and a wool ski cap. On his face was a look of terror that Aaron knew he would never forget.

Aaron stared in horror at the bed sheet that was wrapped around one of the man's hands. It was almost completely scarlet.

In seconds, the policemen pushed the man into the car. One of the policemen walked up to Aaron and Mrs. Findley.

"What's going on?" Aaron asked.

"He was trying to rob your house, son. We took this from him," the officer added, holding up a large pistol.

Aaron looked at the gun in disbelief.

"But how did you know to come?" Aaron asked.

"Dr. Hernandez called us and said we'd better get right over here," the officer said.

"I still don't understand," answered Aaron.

"Look, son, your dog will be fine," continued the policeman. "She wasn't bleeding internally or anything. The vet said she was choking, though."

"Choking?" Aaron wondered. "On what?"

The officer looked back over his shoulder at the police car that held the robber. Then he answered, "She was choking on two human fingers."

Terror Trip

JENNIFER couldn't wait until their summer vacation! Usually, the Smith family spent only a couple weeks at the ocean or in the mountains. But this summer Jennifer was going to travel with her parents clear across the country to Disneyland. It seemed too good to be true—a whole month of vacation!

Jennifer didn't have to wait long. Before she knew it, the car was packed up, and they were ready to go. They spent the first day of their trip on the road, singing silly songs at the top of their lungs. After spending the night at a hotel and swimming in the indoor pool, the family hit the road again.

It was in the middle of the Badlands in South Dakota, on a long, deserted stretch of highway, that they started to hear it. It was a tapping sound from underneath the car that grew louder and louder the faster they went.

Soon the tapping became a pounding.

"What on earth is that?" asked Mr. Smith. "It sounds like we ran over something big."

He pulled the car over to the side of the road and got out. He checked under the car, but there was nothing there. Then he looked up at the sky. Dark clouds were forming, and the wind was blowing harder.

"I think there's going to be a storm," he told Jennifer and her mother.

They started on the road again, but soon Mr. Smith could barely steer the car. He had to stop again. "It feels like there's something caught under the car wheels," said Mrs. Smith.

"But there isn't," answered Jennifer's dad. "I checked."

They stopped the car, just as big raindrops started to hit the windshield. There were no gas stations in sight. In fact, there was nothing around except an old house on a hill next to the highway.

"Let's make a run for it," Mr. Smith said to Jennifer and her mom. "Maybe the people in that house can call a gas station for us."

So, they ran off in the direction of the old house. They got to the porch just in time to beat the storm. As they knocked on the front door, the rain started pouring, and thunder crashed above them.

Jennifer was glad when a girl about her own age opened the door. *At least now I'll have someone to play with,* she thought, *especially if we're stuck here for a long time.*

But she noticed there was something a little strange about the girl. Her eyes seemed to look far away into the distance, down toward the road, when she talked to Jennifer. And then there was the red ribbon she wore around her neck. *Why would anyone wear a fancy ribbon with a T-shirt and jeans?* Jennifer wondered.

But soon Jennifer forgot about it. The girl, whose name was Shelley, asked them into the living room of the old house. Shelley was 10 years old, the same age as Jennifer.

"I live here with my dad," explained Shelley. "Here he comes now."

Shelley's father, Mr. Davidson, came into the living room then and shook hands with the visitors. He offered them some soft drinks. Jennifer noticed something unusual about Shelley's dad, too. He wore a thin bow tie under his sweatshirt—the kind of bow tie a gentleman would wear to a formal occasion. *It looks pretty weird with a sweatshirt,* thought Jennifer. *Oh, well,* Jennifer decided, *maybe it's some funny game they like to play.*

"The phones are out," Mr. Davidson said when he came back with the drinks. "We get lots of storms like this in the summer. Sometimes the electricity goes out, too."

"Is there any way to get a mechanic out here to give us some help?" Mr. Smith asked.

"I don't think so," Mr. Davidson said, shaking his head. "The closest garage is in Pailey, and that's some 40 miles from here. We'll have to wait out the storm. Then you and I can take a look at that engine of yours."

The rain and wind whirled around outside, and the two girls sat in a corner and talked. It turned out they liked the same things— scary books, shopping, soccer, and boys—at least some boys. Jennifer felt lucky that she had found a girl who was so much like herself. Before long, the two were giggling and sharing secrets like they'd known each other a lifetime.

When the rain stopped, their dads headed down the hillside to the car. When Mr. Smith put his key in the ignition, the car started right up. He drove around for a while, and the car didn't seem to shake at all. Whatever that pounding had been, it was gone now.

Jennifer didn't want to leave, but she got Shelley's address and promised to write. The Smiths drove off to begin their vacation, but

Jennifer couldn't stop thinking about the new friend she had made. Sometimes she wondered about the ribbon and the faraway look in Shelley's eyes, but mostly she remembered what a good time they'd had together.

After a great vacation, it was now time for Jennifer's family to go home. When they were driving through the Badlands, Jennifer begged her parents to stop at the Davidsons'. "I'd just like to see Shelley one more time," she pleaded.

"Well, I guess we can," said her mother. "We're going right by their house."

But when the Smiths came to the stretch of road where their car had broken down, they became confused. They remembered that the house was at the end of the long highway just before the turnoff to Pailey. All they saw now was an old, two-room house that was little more than a shack.

"Dad, let's stop and ask," Jennifer begged. "These people will know where the Davidsons' house is."

They stopped at the little house to ask directions. They knocked on the door. Someone inside opened the door just a little and peered out like a frightened animal. When the door opened the rest of the way, Jennifer was surprised to see a woman who looked a lot like

Shelley, only older. The woman looked a little crazy, her black hair falling every which way. The woman invited the family in. But when she heard what they wanted, her face went pale.

"The house you're looking for is just on the other side of the hill," she said. "But you won't find the Davidsons there. No one lives there now. I should know. I'm Mrs. Davidson."

"And you have a daughter named Shelley?" asked Jennifer.

The woman just stared at Jennifer like she was babbling nonsense.

"We met her," continued Jennifer, "and her dad. We had this pounding sound under our car, and we had to stop and—"

Mrs. Davidson cut Jennifer off in mid-sentence. "You couldn't have met my Shelley," the woman said in a loud, but quivering voice.

She paused. Jennifer could see the tears forming in the woman's frightened eyes.

"I told her not to play on the road. I told her that a hundred times..."

Mrs. Smith nodded her head toward the door. "Jennifer, maybe we should go," she said.

"No!" Mrs. Davidson shouted. "No! If you've seen Shelley, if you've seen my husband, we must..."

"Ma'am, are you all right?" asked Mr. Smith.

Mrs. Davidson began sobbing and rocking back and forth. Jennifer felt very sorry for the woman.

Between her sobs, the woman explained, "You see, Shelley wasn't supposed to play in the road. I had come home from shopping that day. There was a bad ice storm, and I didn't see her playing by the road—until it was too late." The woman let out a heartbreaking scream as she said the words.

"I heard a pounding, a terrible pounding sound coming from underneath the car."

She took a deep breath. Jennifer could see she was shaking like a leaf.

"And then I saw my husband running toward the car, waving his hands. But I couldn't stop. The car hit a patch of ice and slid. I'll never get that terrible pounding sound out of my head as long as I live."

The woman's horrified eyes looked out toward the highway.

"Don't you understand? I killed them both! They were caught under my car, and I dragged them. They were making that horrible pounding sound." Then the woman's voice dropped to a whisper.

"Their heads were caught under my wheels," she said. "I chopped their heads off,

44

my own husband and daughter."

"No!" screamed Jennifer. She ran out the front door of the house, running harder than she ever had before. She ran toward where Mrs. Davidson had said the house was, on the other side of the hill. With every step she took, she breathed the words, "No, it can't be true."

Finally, Jennifer reached the house. There it was, standing on the hill just like she remembered it. Jennifer ran toward the door. She knew if she just knocked, Shelley Davidson would open the door and invite her in, just like before. They'd talk and play just like before. That woman had to be crazy. Shelley was here, she knew it.

Trembling, Jennifer reached for the door knocker that hung on the front door. But before she could knock, she saw something hanging on the doorknob.

It was the red ribbon, and next to it, the bow tie. Jennifer reached for them with her trembling hand.

The next sound Jennifer heard was the sound of her own scream. As she turned the ribbon and the bow tie over in her hands, she saw that each was covered with fresh blood.

The Last Initiation

DARREN had always dreamed about being a member of Alpha Beta Delta. It was the best fraternity at his college. All the neatest guys belonged to it. That's why he was so happy when he received the letter asking if he wanted to join. He had gone to several meetings and had passed all the interviews. Now the only thing left for him was the fraternity initiation.

He wasn't too worried about it. After all, a lot of other guys had survived the initiation and gotten into Alpha Beta Delta. Anyway, he was so excited about being chosen for the fraternity that he was willing to do anything.

Darren was to meet the fraternity brothers at the edge of town. Then they would walk to the house of Jeremiah Stone, an abandoned old mansion that was about to fall down. He guessed that he would have to pass some kind of scary trial. And then he'd be a member of the best fraternity at Hines College!

Darren was right. On a cloudy, windy night, a group of about 10 guys met him on the edge of campus. Together they walked the mile or so through the woods to the old mansion. On the way, Scott, the president of the fraternity, told him about Jeremiah Stone and the legends of the old house.

"Jeremiah Stone was a banker in town," explained Scott. "When it was discovered that a large amount of money was missing from his bank, he vanished from sight. He was found a week later up in the very tower where you will have to prove you are worthy to become a member of Alpha Beta Delta. Jeremiah Stone had hanged himself."

Darren looked up to see the moon rising over the trees. The moon was just about full.

"Ever since that dreadful night they discovered the banker," continued Scott, "the people in town have avoided the old mansion. People say it's haunted. Some people even say that they have seen strange lights in the dark tower, especially on nights like this. And some claim to have heard sounds, unearthly, inhuman sounds, coming from the tower room where..."

Here Scott paused.

Boy, thought Darren, *these guys are really playing it up. I can't believe Scott can keep a straight face.*

"...where he is," Scott finished.

When the group came out of the woods, Darren saw ahead of him, a huge gray, tumbledown house. Windows were broken. Shutters hung down flapping in the wind. And dead leaves raced by as the wind gusted. The whole house looked rotten enough to fall down any minute.

And there, reaching high into the gloomy night sky, was the tower. When the moon came out from behind a cloud, Darren could see a window near the top of the tower.

The group gathered around him, looking serious.

Then Scott said in a low voice, "Darren Richardson, to prove you are worthy to become a brother of Alpha Beta Delta, here is what you must do. You must climb the stairs to the haunted tower in darkness."

One of the guys handed Scott an old oil lamp and a box of matches.

"You will light this lamp when you reach the top," continued Scott solemnly. "You will show the lamp at the window, and we will know you have passed the final initiation test. Do you understand?"

"Yes," answered Darren.

"One more thing," said Scott. "You must never reveal to anyone what you see and hear in the haunted tower. Swear by the ghost of Jeremiah Stone."

Oh, come on, thought Darren. *Give me a break.* But he said nothing and swore he would not tell.

Scott walked with Darren to the porch of the old mansion. Several boards had rotted away, and Darren had to be careful not to fall right through.

"Remember," said Scott, "do not light the lamp until you reach the tower."

When Scott opened the door for Darren to enter, it creaked. And when Scott slammed the door closed, Darren was alone inside the mansion.

He looked around. Even though he had no light, the moon shone through the many holes and broken windows in the house. Darren could see old broken furniture that looked like it would collapse if anyone touched it, dirty old paintings, even some glasses and plates on a table. And there were dust and cobwebs everywhere.

On the other side of the large hallway, he saw the staircase that he thought must lead up to the tower. Now that he was alone in the dark house, he didn't feel quite so brave about the whole thing.

"Well," he said to himself loudly to perk up his spirits, "I might as well get going. It's just an old house. I don't believe in ghosts. That's ridiculous."

Taking his first step toward the stairs, he heard a scurrying sound near his foot. Just then, a large rat scampered across a patch of moonlight. Darren cried out and shivered.

"Oh, come on. Pull yourself together. It's just a rat," he said to himself.

Guided by the moonlight, Darren worked his way slowly up the first steps. He didn't want to touch the railing, not knowing what his hand might feel. He remembered the huge rat and all the cobwebs.

After his eyes got used to the dim light, Darren found that he could see well enough to make his way. When he came to the second floor landing, he looked out a broken window. Below, he saw Scott and the others standing in the moonlight.

Higher and higher he climbed. Sometimes when the moon went behind a cloud, Darren found himself in almost total darkness. He wished he could light a match. But maybe they would see it from down below, and he'd fail the trial.

From outside, he had guessed that the tower room was three stories high. But now he was on the stairs to the fourth floor, and he still had some way to go. He felt a little out of breath and paused to rest in the darkness.

Then he heard it.

It started as a low moaning, coming from somewhere up above. It got louder and softer. Then it stopped completely.

Darren decided that it must have been his imagination playing tricks on him and started up the stairs again. When he had reached the fourth floor landing, with one flight of steps to go to the tower, he froze. Somewhere above him, he heard a thud and something breaking, and then a soft choking sound. Then everything was quiet. He heard only the wind blowing through the cracks in the walls.

Something in Darren made him want to turn around and go back down the stairs, get out of this house, and never come near it again. But then he thought about how much he wanted to be an Alpha Beta Delta, how it had always been his dream. He also thought about how Scott and the others might laugh at him for running away—from something that was probably just his imagination.

Darren took a deep breath and started up

again. He felt the matches in his pocket.

At the very top of the staircase, he found a closed door. *This has to lead to the tower room,* he thought. *This is where the banker hanged himself.* He pushed at the door. It slowly creaked open.

Peering inside, Darren saw a small room with some broken furniture. There was only one window—the window he had to shine the lamp from. It was dark in the room. The moon wasn't shining in the single window.

As Darren walked slowly across the room, he reached in his pocket for the matches. *In 10 seconds,* he told himself, *I'll shine the lamp out the window, and I'll be an Alpha Beta Delta.*

He struck the match and lighted the lamp. He held it out to light up the small tower room.

Then he screamed like he had never screamed before.

In the darkest corner of the room was a body hanging from a beam in the ceiling. It was dressed in a dark suit, like a banker.

Darren ran from the room screaming. He tore down the steps as fast as his legs would carry him. Several times he almost tripped. But the terrible sight he had seen was burned in his brain. And he imagined the cold grip of the dead man's hands on the back of his own neck.

When he finally burst out into the open air, he collapsed on the ground. He shut his eyes to try to get rid of the dreadful sight of the ghost of the hanged man. But it wouldn't go away.

Then he quickly looked up. He was surrounded by Scott and the others. They were laughing hysterically.

"What's going on?" Darren demanded.

"You should have seen your face!" shouted Scott through tears of laughter. "I've never seen anything so funny in my life."

"But...but...I saw the banker, a gho..."

"You saw Don McLoughlin, one of us, dressed like a banker!" shouted Scott. "He was pretending to be hanged!"

The others laughed even louder. Darren stood up, starting to get the idea.

"Come on," said Scott. "We'll show you."

They all turned on their flashlights and started into the old house and up the stairs.

"But it looked so real," muttered Darren.

"Sure it looked real," answered one of the guys. "Don's an acting major. He knows all about costumes and makeup."

They ran quickly up the stairs to the tower, laughing and teasing Darren about the great joke they played on him.

Darren had started to feel a little better. He was now one of the guys.

Scott opened the door to the tower, and they all burst into the room shouting and congratulating Don on his great job.

But the laughter turned to stunned horror when they shined their flashlights into the darkest corner of the room. There, three feet above a broken, rotted chair that he had been standing on, dangled Don's lifeless body.

The Rose Garden

W HEN Cassie Johnson was a little girl, the thing she loved best was to visit her grandmother and grandfather at their farm. She always felt happiest when she was walking through the woods and fields, or swinging on the porch swing on the big front porch. She had never felt so safe and warm as she did at her grandparents' farm.

Other times she would sit in the cozy kitchen while her grandmother baked. Cassie spent long, wonderful hours smelling the rich smell of oatmeal cookies baking in the oven, and listening to the wonderful stories her grandmother told.

Cassie especially liked hearing about the old days, when her grandparents were young and had first moved to the area of Ohio that would be their home for the rest of their lives. In those days, her grandmother told her, the area was mostly woods. She and Cassie's grandfather had had to clear away an area for their house and then, little by little, an area for the farm.

"I didn't want the house down here in the valley, child," her grandmother said with a hint of mischief in her eyes. "I wanted it up on that hill so I could see the world and everything that went on. And I wanted the house to face the south, so I would have enough sun to grow my roses."

Cassie's grandmother looked through the window toward the distant hill. "I just didn't think I could live out here without my yellow roses," she added with a gentle smile.

"Oh, pooh," Cassie's grandfather said, his blue eyes twinkling. "We needed the house here so we could be closer to water, you know that. Roses! Ha!" he said with a laugh and a shake of his gray head.

Cassie knew that her grandparents weren't really fighting. It was just an old joke between them. She had heard the two of them joke goodnaturedly about it for years. It was part of what she liked so much about visiting them. They told the same stories every time and had the same old arguments. Nothing ever seemed to change.

Determined, her grandmother had tried to

go ahead and grow her yellow roses, anyway. But down in the valley, behind the old farmhouse, the roses never got enough sun, and they were always small and sickly. Even though they were never very healthy, Cassie's grandmother loved her yellow roses. She pruned them carefully with her special long-handled gardening shears.

Cassie remembered the time that her grandmother placed the shears in her hands and taught her how to cut with them. "Maybe someday, you'll learn to love these roses as much as I do, Cassie," her grandmother said.

* * * * *

It happened one winter day when Cassie was in school a hundred miles from her grandparents' farm. The farmhouse caught fire. People said that maybe it had started in the barn in the straw. Or, maybe there had been a short in the wiring of the old house somewhere. Cassie didn't want to know the details. The only thing she knew was that the fire had burned down the wonderful old farmhouse where she had spent so many happy times. And her grandparents had perished in the blaze.

Cassie never went to look at the charred

ruins of the place she loved. And it was years before she could face the deaths of her two favorite people in the world. She grew up, as all little girls do, but she never forgot those wonderful days at the farm. And she never found that warm, safe feeling that she had there anywhere else. But at last, when she became a teenager, she was finally able to think of them without crying.

One day, she and her boyfriend were driving through the same area where her grandparents' old farm had stood.

"Cassie," her boyfriend said, "I can't believe you've never gone back to the place where the farm was. We're so close now, let's go take a look."

"Well, okay," she answered. "Maybe it would be nice to see it after all this time."

She saw the sign for McConnellsville, and they turned off the main highway. They headed down the old dirt road that led to the farm property.

But when they pulled up the drive to where the farmhouse had stood, Cassie couldn't believe her eyes. There was no sign of the house in the valley. There was no foundation, no burned, ruined building—nothing. It was as if the farm had never been there. Stunned, she looked at her boyfriend, who stood shaking his head slowly.

"Come on, Cassie," he said. "You must have gotten mixed up. It's obvious no one ever lived here. Maybe we got off at the wrong exit."

Cassie nodded, the tears welling up in her eyes, and headed back to the car.

"Hey," said her boyfriend, "since we're here, why don't we take a walk up that hill? I bet the view is great from up there."

"Well, okay," she answered. "I just don't understand why there's no sign at all of the house."

They walked up the hill together. Cassie became quiet and thoughtful. Now that she was here again after all these years, the wonderful memories came back, more real than ever. She almost expected to hear her grandparents' voices calling her and see them walking across the fields hand in hand. But, she remembered sadly, that it could never be. They were gone. And now, she thought, there's not even any sign of the farmhouse.

Her boyfriend had run on ahead to the top of the hill while Cassie had stopped to look back down into the valley. Suddenly, she heard his voice calling, breaking into her sad daydream about her grandparents.

"Cassie!" he shouted from the top of the hill. "Come on up here."

She jogged up the rest of the way. *I knew Mike would like the view from up there,* she thought.

"See. I told you you were mixed up," Mike said as Cassie came up to the top. "The house was obviously up here, on this hill. Look. There's the foundation of the house and the ruins." He pointed toward the center of the hill, where an old charred foundation was clearly visible.

"But it can't be," Cassie said as she walked toward the foundation. "There's got to be some..."

Then she saw them.

On the other side of the foundation, behind some weeds and bushes, were five of the most beautiful yellow rose bushes Cassie had ever seen. Their beautiful blossoms took her breath away.

She and Mike approached the rose bushes, breathing in their heavenly scent.

"I'll pick one for you," said Mike, reaching toward the bushes. But his hand stopped short of the rose blossom.

"What's this?" he asked.

Cassie looked. There on the ground lay her grandmother's special long-handled pruning shears. And next to the shears was a perfect yellow rose, recently plucked.

Cassie kneeled and picked up the rose. She held it in her hand and said softly, "Grandmother got her wish. The house is finally where she wanted it to be."

The Man on the Dock

CRAIG and Mark left their bikes at the bait store steps and went in to borrow one of Mr. Easom's canoes.

"We just want to use it for the morning, Mr. Easom. We have to be back by 2:00 for swim team practice," said Craig.

"Okay, boys, but be careful of the currents out there. The water's a little high after all this rain," Mr. Easom warned. "But the fishing should be great."

Craig and Mark loaded the boat with their gear and bait. They noticed a strange man standing near the dock. He waved them over. Mark put down his bait pail and started to go over to the man. But Craig stopped him.

"What are you doing? We don't know that guy," Craig said. "We don't have time to hang around here and talk to him and still get back in time for practice. And besides," Craig said, "he looks kind of weird."

Mark and Craig looked at the man. He was wearing a muddy, old white shirt that stuck to his skin as if it were wet. The collar was buttoned up around his neck in spite of the heat of the morning. When the man saw the boys looking at him, he motioned to them again.

"But maybe he's from around here and knows a good place to fish," Mark said. "Come on. Let's go talk to him."

"Well, all right," Craig gave in. "But let's hurry."

"Hey," Mark said as he approached the man.

"Hello," answered the man in a thin voice. "Where are you boys going fishing?" he asked.

"Oh, probably at Bridger's Branch," Mark said. "We're kind of new in town."

"I see," said the man, looking at the boys. "You're new in town, are you?"

"Yeah. Have you been out fishing already this morning?" Craig asked. He wanted to ask the man if he fell in the lake, but decided not to.

"Yes, that's right," the man said. "I was out on the lake with my friends. We haven't caught anything yet, but I think we will soon. I think our luck is turning."

"Well, where's the best place to fish?" Craig asked. "Where are you and your friends fishing?" Craig eyed the man carefully. He seemed awfully thin and boney, and his face was pale. Craig wondered how anyone could be so pale at the end of the summer.

"We're fishing over near the flooded locust grove," the man said in his thin voice. "It's on the other side of the lake. That's where my friends and I are. There are lots of fish over there—big ones, too. I'll give you directions how to get there."

"Hey, Craig, let's try it," Mark said, turning toward his friend. "We've never been to that part of the lake. Uh, Craig?"

But Craig was already walking back toward the boat.

"Come on, Mark," Craig said impatiently. "Let's get going. We don't have time to talk." And under his breath, he added, "Especially to some weirdo."

"Listen," said Mark, "you go get the boat ready, and I'll ask this guy more about his good place to fish. I'll be there in a minute."

After a few minutes, Mark joined Craig at the boat. "Craig, that man said he caught a 12-inch bass near that flooded grove. Come on. Let's go over there."

"Okay, okay," answered Craig. "I don't care

where we fish. Let's just get going so we don't have to turn around and come right back."

As the boys paddled away from the dock, they looked back at the old man. He was waving at them. They heard his thin voice floating over the water to them. "Good luck, boys," the old man called to them. "I know you'll have good luck."

It took the boys about a half an hour to reach the secluded cove where the old man said they would have good luck. The opening to the cove was partly hidden by overgrown trees and bushes. But the old man's directions had been perfect, and Mark was able to find it.

"Hmm," Craig said, "I guess this does look like a pretty good place, after all. There could be a lot of fish in here."

"See, I told you we were right to listen to that guy," said Mark. "He just looked like he spent a lot of time on the lake. He knew what he was talking about."

The boys paddled under the overhanging branches into the cove. The trees hanging over the water almost blocked the sky.

"It's kind of dark in here," said Mark. "The fish will be coming to the surface. I have a feeling this is going to be our lucky day."

The surface of the water was scattered with

tree limbs, and old rotting boards. Dead tree branches stuck out of the water like boney hands reaching up toward the cloudy sky.

The boys threw in their lines and fished in the gloomy spot about an hour. They caught nothing. "Maybe that guy's tip wasn't so great, after all," Craig said.

"Let's try one more cast," said Mark. "I can't believe this place isn't jumping with fish. It looks perfect."

After a few minutes, Mark's line snapped tight in the water, and something tugged hard below the murky surface of the cove.

"All right! I finally got a bite!" Mark shouted. He was so excited that he stood up suddenly in the canoe. He was trying to hold on to the line. But the fish on the end was pulling away quickly.

Craig yelled, "Mark, sit down! You're rocking the boat!"

But his warning was too late. Mark was pulled right into the dark water of the lake. He popped up a few seconds later.

"It's not a fish at all, Craig," he said, disappointed. "It looks like my line's caught on a big box or something. I'll unhook it."

Craig shouted at him to just leave it there. But Mark had already dived under the water. When the water's surface began to ripple and churn, Craig expected Mark to pop back up near the canoe any second. But when Mark did not come up, Craig began to get worried. He reached his hand over the side into the water, hoping Mark would see his hand.

The water was icy cold!

How can the water be so cold? thought Craig. *It's the middle of August!* As he clutched the side of the canoe, Craig was suddenly very afraid. Something was wrong, really wrong. His mind went back to the strange man on the dock. He shivered to think of the man's thin voice and strange, pale appearance.

"Mark! Mark!" called Craig hysterically. The only sound was the echo of his voice and the dark water slapping against the black branches. Craig didn't know what to do. Mark had been under the water for about five minutes. And Mark was a better swimmer than Craig was. If Mark couldn't get free, what could *he* do? If Craig dove in, he might get caught, too. He grabbed quickly at the paddles and began to back the canoe out of the snarl of branches and into open water. He rowed as hard as he could, but it seemed like he wasn't getting anywhere. It almost seemed like something was holding the canoe in the dark cove.

With a powerful push against a fallen tree, he paddled out of the cove into the main part of the lake. Turning back to take a final look for his friend, Craig saw something floating on the surface of the water. It was Mark's baseball cap. With a scream, Craig started paddling as fast as he could across the lake toward the dock.

Back at the dock, Mr. Easom called the police immediately. When they arrived, they took out a map of the lake so Craig could show them exactly where Mark had disappeared.

"It's the flooded locust grove," Craig said frantically, pointing to the map. "A man on the dock told us about it. He said he and his friends had caught lots of fish over there."

Mr. Easom's face turned white. "A man on the dock told you that? And he told you to fish there?"

"Yes," Craig said. "What's wrong? Why are you looking at me like that?"

"Was it an old man with wet clothes and a strange, thin voice?" asked the oldest policeman.

"Yeah," answered Craig. "That's him. He looked like he's been around this lake for a long time."

The policeman looked at Mr. Easom. "He probably has," said the policeman.

Mr. Easom shook his head. "Craig, 30 years ago, that area where you were fishing was flooded to make the lake larger," he explained. "A few days after the water had covered up the land, people started to notice big boxes floating in the water."

"We saw boards, but I still don't understand," Craig said. "What does that have to do with Mark?"

"The area that was flooded was the old prison graveyard," explained the policeman. "It's where they buried the murderers who were hanged. People around here call it Dead Man's Cove. And they say the boards over there are from the hanged men's coffins."

"And you didn't know because you're new here," said Mr. Easom sadly.

"Mark is the seventh person in 30 years to disappear there," said the policeman. "We've never found any of the bodies. And each time it's happened, the survivors said an old man told them to go fishing in the cove."

"But what about the old man?" Craig asked. "Why don't you arrest him?"

The policeman sighed and touched Craig's arm. "Because the man on the dock bears a very strong resemblance to old Willie Marolf, a murderer who was hanged and buried there 60 years ago."

The Hitchhiker

MAGGIE had just gotten her driver's license. She was excited that her mother had agreed to let her take the car to the mall on Saturday afternoon. She could shop all day if she wanted to. It was fantastic. She had never known such a feeling of freedom before.

Before she left, her mother gave her a long list of instructions. "Now, just remember what you learned in driving school, Maggie," her mother explained. "There's a lot of traffic at the mall. And remember what your father and I told you about not picking up any strange hitchhikers."

"I know, Mom," said Maggie impatiently. She couldn't wait to get going.

"You know how many weirdos there are hanging around the mall parking lot. Be careful," her mother added.

"I'll be careful, Mom," said Maggie. "Don't

worry. I *am* 16, you know."

When her mom was finally finished talking, Maggie grabbed her purse and ran out to the car. She could hear the keys jingling in her purse as she ran. She flew out of the driveway and was off!

Maggie shopped all afternoon and long into the evening. She even ran into some school friends at the mall and had a quick dinner with them. It was already dark when she headed for the car, loaded down with bags and boxes.

As she got near her parents' car, she was surprised to see a tall elderly woman step out of a shadow into the light. She heard the lady calling to her. "Oh, young lady, Miss!"

The woman had white hair and wore those old-fashioned shoes that looked a little like men's loafers. *She walks pretty quickly for an old person*, Maggie thought.

"Yes?" Maggie answered as the woman came closer. "Is there something wrong?"

"Oh, no, dear. Well, maybe there is," the old woman said. "My car doesn't seem to want to start no matter what I do. I was wondering if you'd be nice enough to give me a ride to my daughter's house." The woman looked around the parking lot and then added, "I've seen several men go by, but you know a woman just can't be too careful these days. I thought another woman would understand. And it would be safer, don't you think?"

Maggie thought for a moment. She remembered what her mother had said about not picking up hitchhikers. She'd never pick up some tough-looking man. But this old woman was obviously in trouble. How would the woman get to her daughter's house if Maggie didn't help her? She sure couldn't walk. And besides, there was something about her that reminded Maggie of her own grandmother.

"Sure, I'll take you to your daughter's house," said Maggie with a smile. "Why don't you just go around to the passenger's side. I'll unlock the door from the inside."

The old woman moved to the other side of the car quickly. *She gets around pretty well for her age*, Maggie thought again. As she fumbled with the lock on the inside, Maggie noticed that the old lady's hands on the door handle seemed awfully large for a woman's hands. *Maybe she did some heavy work when she was younger*, Maggie thought.

As the old woman got into the car, Maggie could see in the lighted front seat that the woman was indeed tall. Her head almost touched the car ceiling, like her dad's did. And her dad was six feet two. *Maybe this lady was a basketball player*, Maggie thought with a laugh.

As the old woman settled into the seat, her eyes met Maggie's. She must have noticed Maggie staring at her hands, because she pulled on a pair of white gloves. They were longer and seemed shinier somehow than the kind Maggie had seen her aunts wear. "Oh, those gloves are different," Maggie said, trying to make conversation.

"Yes, these are special gloves," the old woman said, staring now at Maggie.

Maggie thought it was weird that the woman didn't explain what she meant by "special." As she reached to pull on her seat belt, she began to feel uncomfortable that the old lady was watching her so carefully.

"Uh, where exactly does your daughter live?" Maggie nervously asked the old lady.

"Oh, if you just pull out on the highway, I'll show you where it is," the old lady said, pointing toward the road. In the light of a street lamp, Maggie caught a glimpse of the old woman's bare arm as she pointed toward the highway. The woman's arm was large and hairy!

"Oh, you know, I—uh—think I forgot something at the mall," Maggie said suddenly. Before the woman could say a word, Maggie opened the door and jumped from the car. She slipped the car keys into her coat pocket.

"If I forget the dry cleaning, my mom will strangle me. I'll be back as soon as I can. You can just wait here. Okay?" she shouted back through the open car door.

It took every ounce of courage she had for Maggie not to run toward the mall. When she went up to the security guard and told him she needed help, she could barely catch her breath to talk. "Please, help me," she said between gasps. "There's a strange person in my car," she gushed.

The passenger was still sitting in the front seat when Maggie and three guards came back. A policeman was with them.

"Okay, out of the car, NOW!" shouted one of the guards. "Put your hands up!" The men threw open the car door and aimed their guns at the woman. She looked at all of them with the eyes of a trapped beast. She snarled and shrieked in a way that gave Maggie chills of fright. Then the old woman sprang at them like a savage animal, trying to hit one of the guards with her purse.

Maggie screamed.

But the guards quickly wrestled the passenger to the ground. The policeman grabbed the woman's hair and yanked it off. It was a wig! They put handcuffs around the large, hairy wrists.

"Hey, what's going on?" asked one of the guards. "Those are surgical gloves, the kind doctors wear for operations." The man on the ground was whimpering like a hurt animal.

The police officer lifted up the purse, and the man let out a blood-curdling howl. The policeman reached into the purse. The last thing Maggie remembered before she fainted was the policeman lifting out a long, shiny scalpel.

Trick or Treat

DAVID and Scott Marcus weren't very happy about having to take their six-year-old sister Katie trick or treating with them.

"Mom! She'll slow us down," complained David, who was 13. "She takes forever to walk up to each house."

"Yeah," added Scott, who was 11. "We won't be able to get to as many houses. And besides, she'll stop and talk to people. You know how friendly she is."

"I don't want to hear you guys complain," said their mother sternly as they were getting ready to go out. "She's your little sister, for heaven's sake. Do you want her to go trick or treating all by herself, with all the strange people around at night?"

"Aw, come on, Mom," said Scott. "There aren't any strange people here in Northridge. It's only a little town. We know almost everybody around here."

"The discussion is over," said their mom. "Katie goes with you guys, and that's final. Be careful, and keep an eye on your sister."

"Okay," David grumbled. "Come on, Katie. Let's go."

The three of them worked their way down the street, stopping at each house. The jack o' lanterns were glowing. The sounds of children screaming and laughing filled the neighborhood. The weather was perfect for trick or treating—warm enough so they didn't have to wear coats over their costumes. Scott was dressed as a mummy. David was dressed as a football player. And Katie was dressed as a princess.

As they headed down the block, they met other kids and admired their costumes. Sometimes they would walk along with some of the kids they met. Usually they recognized their friends because they had talked at school about what they were going to be that night for Halloween.

They had been out about half an hour, and their bags were getting full. Katie had actually been pretty good. She hadn't whined and was keeping up with her older brothers. They were on the lighted porch of the Links' house, several blocks away from home, on the edge of Turner's Woods. All three of them stuck their bags through the opened door and shouted, "Trick or treat!"

Mr. Link dropped a candy bar into each of the bags. He chuckled to himself, "Those are great costumes, kids." Then he added, "Here's one for your big brother back there."

David turned around confused. Scott said to Mr. Link, "But my big brother's right here."

But Katie shouted to the figure in the shadows, "Come on. Don't be afraid. You say 'trick or treat,' and they give you candy."

When the figure retreated back from the porch light, Katie grabbed the candy bar and took it to the person standing on the edge of the darkness.

"Thank you, Mr. Link," said the boys, and they followed Katie down the sidewalk. They got a closer look at the figure. It was a person dressed in a white sheet like a ghost, with a string tied loosely around the neck. There were eyeholes and a mouth cut in the sheet. The person began eating the candy bar that Katie had given him.

"Hi," said Scott.

"Hi," said the ghost and looked away shyly.

"That's a good costume," said David.

"Thanks," said the ghost.

The group walked along together to the

next house. Under the streetlight, David and Scott studied their new friend. *He's pretty tall for a kid*, thought David. *And he walks sort of funny.* He was wearing white tennis shoes and white pants—to go with the ghost costume, decided David.

"Here, ghost," Katie was saying. "You don't have a trick or treat bag, so you can share mine."

"Thank you, Katie," answered the ghost. "You're a nice little girl to share with me."

As they walked along, David and Scott went up to each house to trick or treat. The ghost didn't like to go up to the porches, so he started to wait at the sidewalk, and the boys would bring him candy. Katie waited at the sidewalk, chattering away happily to her new friend.

"Hey, David," whispered Scott. "Do you think maybe we should get away from that kid. I don't recognize him."

"I think it's okay. Besides, I know who he is," said his brother. "I think he's a ninth grader at my school. I recognize his voice. Anyway, he's looking after Katie, so we can go to more houses."

The four of them wandered from house to house, collecting more and more candy. The sky had clouded over, making a ring around the moon. It was getting darker, and the boys began to think about heading home. The wind had started to blow and whip the bare branches around. They looked like wild, boney fingers reaching for the sky.

"Hey, ghost," Katie was saying as they walked on the sidewalk along the edge of Turner's Woods. "The moon is spooky, isn't it? I like Halloween."

"I do, too," said the ghost. "It's my favorite time of the year."

"Ghost," said Katie, "will you carry my bag? It's too heavy."

"Sure, I will," answered the ghost.

After another half an hour, David said, "I guess we better get back home."

"Yeah," added Scott. Turning to the ghost, he said, "We'll see you around. It was nice trick or treating with you."

The ghost waved his hand, and Katie waved back. "See you next Halloween," she called cheerfully.

"See you next Halloween," echoed the ghost. The three children watched as he walked off into Turner's Woods.

"He walks funny," said Katie. "But he's nice."

"Did he tell you what his name was?" asked Scott.

"Yeah, he did," answered Katie. "But I forget what it was. Let's go home. I'm cold."

"Come on!" shouted Scott. "Let's run!"

The three ran through the streets toward home, excited about finally being able to look at all their candy. The boys ran slowly so their little sister could keep up. When they reached their house, they were out of breath from laughing and running. They burst through the front door, threw off their masks, and began telling their mother and father all about what they had done and seen on that Halloween night.

"I met a nice ghost!" shouted Katie. "He carried my trick or treat bag for me."

"I think he's a ninth grader at school," said David.

"Well, it sounds like you had a great time," said their mother. "Come on in, and get warm by the fireplace."

Their parents were watching TV in the living room. The children emptied their Halloween bags, each in a corner of the room. They laughed and shouted as they showed each other their best things.

"I got 17 chocolate bars!" announced Scott.

"I got two popcorn balls," added Katie.

David crawled over to Katie's pile of candy and pretended to steal some. She squealed.

"I'm going to take your...hey, what's this?" David asked, holding up a little metal tag on a broken chain that he pulled from his sister's candy pile. "Katie, where did you get this?"

"That's my necklace. Give it back," she said, grabbing for the chain and taking it back.

"Hold it down for a second, kids," said their dad. "They're interrupting the TV show for a special news bulletin."

The family listened to the voice on the TV. There was a picture of a strange-looking man staring blankly out from the screen.

"Murderer William Spires has escaped from the Clintonville State Hospital for the criminally insane. He had been serving a life sentence for the brutal ax murder of 11 people on Halloween night 15 years ago. He is considered extremely dangerous to adults, but some hospital guards report that Spires loves children. He was last seen wearing his white hospital uniform and tennis shoes. He can be identified by his awkward walk and his hospital name tag, number 1287-50. Use extreme caution with this man."

"Katie," said David hoarsely, "let me see your necklace."

"Okay," she answered, "but give it back. The nice ghost gave it to me."

82

David held the metal tag in his trembling hand and showed it to his family. In the light of the fire, they read the numbers on the tag— 1287-50.

It Walks At Midnight

MIKE and Rob loved hiking in the countryside near the college they attended in Kentucky. Along with Mike's dog Ernie, they had been to most of the state parks in their area. But they were especially excited about the next hike they were going to take. They were going to the fantastic Red River Gorge over spring vacation.

"Look at those cliff walls!" said Rob on the hike into the gorge.

"Awesome!" answered Mike. "They're even steeper than I thought they'd be."

After hiking for most of the afternoon, setting up camp, and then fixing dinner, they were pretty tired. Even Ernie, who had been exploring all over, looked beat. They were relaxing around the campfire, looking up at the sky, and listening to the night sounds. The full moon made everything look a little spooky.

Mike tossed another log on the fire. They watched as the sparks floated up into the darkness. Rob reached down to scratch Ernie's ears. But Ernie was gone.

"Hey," asked Rob, "did you hear Ernie run off?"

"No," answered Mike, "but don't worry. He'll come back."

But just then they heard a yelping and whimpering coming from somewhere out in the dark woods. They both recognized Ernie's bark and stood up. Mike grabbed his flashlight and they started walking in the direction of the whimpering.

"Here Ernie, come here, boy," they called.

Soon they heard a rustling sound in the thick underbrush. A minute later, Ernie came bursting out of the bushes and ran toward Mike. The poor dog was trembling all over, and the fur on his back was sticking straight up.

"Hey, what's wrong, Ernie?" asked Mike. "You look like you've seen a ghost." Ernie just whimpered and hid behind Mike's legs.

"Whatever's in there sure scared Ernie," said Rob. "Maybe it's a bear or a wildcat."

Mike shined his flashlight into the dark woods where Ernie had come running out. The shadows of the trees and all the leaves made lots of fantastic shapes.

"Look up there!" whispered Rob, pointing to a small ledge about twenty feet above the ground.

"W-w-what is it?" Mike whispered.

"It's not like any bear I've ever seen," Rob said. "It looks more like a huge black dog."

On the ledge, staring down at them in the moonlight with eyes that seemed to glow like little points of red fire, stood a large black dog.

"Look at the way he's moving his head," Mike said. "It's almost like he's trying to tell us something."

"Yeah, like 'Get out of here!,'" answered Rob. "I think that's pretty good advice."

"No, I don't think so," said Mike. "Look at his eyes. I think he wants us to come with him somewhere."

"You must be kidding. That dog looks like a monster," Rob replied. "Now look what he's doing!"

As Rob and Mike watched in amazement, the huge black dog seemed to float up into the air. It floated back up the side of the cliff wall and, with one final piercing stare down at them, turned and disappeared without a sound. A minute later, they heard a blood-curdling howl from somewhere off in the distance. It sounded half-human, almost like a person crying in agony.

The guys could barely sleep that night, and the next morning they went to the ranger station to report what they had seen. When they had told their story to the ranger, he sighed.

"I'll be honest with you guys," he said. "You aren't the first to report seeing that dog, or whatever it was. The stories are always pretty much the same. And it's always people camping in that area where you guys were. To tell you the truth, I almost expected someone to report it today."

"Why?" asked Mike. "Why today?"

"Because last night was a full moon," the ranger answered. "The creature is only seen on the night of the full moon. Then it disappears."

"Well, do you know what it is?" asked Rob.

"No, we don't. It could be a dog that's gone wild, or a wolf or bear that people didn't get a very good look at. Or," the ranger said after a pause, "it could be a ghost."

"But...," said Mike.

"I know, I don't believe in ghosts either," the ranger said. "But when you're out in the gorge alone on a moonlit night, you start thinking about all the stories and legends you've heard. Sometimes you start to think that anything could happen in there."

Mike and Rob remembered the unearthly howl and the dog's piercing, fiery eyes. Maybe the ranger was right. Anything could happen in there. They were getting up to leave when Mike remembered something.

"Did any of the other people report that the dog seemed to be trying to tell them something?" he asked.

The ranger gave him a serious look. Then he said, "As a matter of fact, another person did notice that the dog seemed to be moving his head in a strange way, like he was trying to point somewhere."

"Yeah, that's what he did," said Mike excitedly.

"That person was me," said the ranger. "After I read some of the reports, I decided to go try to see the thing myself. After seeing it, I didn't know what to think."

"Listen," said Rob, who had been quiet for a while. "Have you checked through old records and reports to see if anybody has lost a dog?"

"Yeah, I looked through all the stuff in my office, which goes back ten years. Anything older than that would be at the district warehouse in Stanford."

"That's where our college is," said Rob. "We could check the old records."

"That would be great," said the ranger, "but the stuff is old and messy. It would be a big job. Those records go back into the last century."

"We'll give it a try," said Mike.

It was a busy time at school, and Rob and Mike didn't have much time for the search. They did finally get to spend a whole Saturday looking through the musty old report files. Farther and farther back in time they went. It was interesting to read about all the different things people had lost throughout the years. Someone in 1928 had lost a Model T Ford!

After six hours of searching and sneezing from all the dust, they were about to give up. Then Mike held up an old yellowed piece of paper with some faded writing on it. "Take a look at this," he said.

The report was from June 22, 1935. It told of a ten-year-old boy who had been camping in the gorge with his family. He wandered off on a rainy evening and never came back. The family and park rangers searched for him, but his body was never found. Stapled to the back of the report was a piece of notebook paper. Mike read it aloud.

"The family's dog, a black Labrador retriever named Midnight, was also never found."

"We have to show this to the ranger!" cried Rob.

* * * * *

They arranged with the ranger to drive out on the afternoon of the next full moon. He met them at the door of the ranger station.

"I checked the almanac for 1935," he said. "June 22 was a full moon."

Together, all three hiked back into the area where Mike and Rob had seen the dog a month earlier. Ernie seemed nervous to be back where he had gotten such a fright. The sky began to cloud over as they set up camp in the same place.

"Looks like it could drizzle," said the ranger.

"It's starting to look like that day in 1935," said Mike. "The report said it was rainy."

Mike, Rob, and the ranger sat quietly after dinner, waiting for something they knew might never show up. Mike didn't know which would be worse—if the dog never appeared, or if it did. Maybe he didn't want to know the dog's strange secret. Maybe it was better to just leave such things alone.

The campfire was burning low. Ernie was sleeping at Mike's feet. It hadn't rained, but the fog and mist had descended into the gorge, making them feel more alone than ever.

Suddenly Ernie's ears pricked up. He sniffed once or twice and then became stiff with fear. He started to tremble and whimper. Mike petted the frightened dog and said softly, "I think it's here."

They all looked up through the mist to the same ledge. There stood the great black dog. The fog made the dog's fiery eyes seem even brighter. Mike tied Ernie's leash to a log and whispered, "Stay here, boy."

Mike, Rob, and the ranger slowly stood up and walked toward the cliff where the dog stood motionless. Through the mist they all noticed again the strange way the dog moved his head. When they were as close to the ledge as they could come without climbing, Mike nodded at Rob. Rob took a deep breath and called out through the mist in a voice made hoarse by fear.

"Midnight! Midnight! Take us where you want us to go. We'll follow you."

What the dog did next sent chills of terror up the spines of all three of them. He turned his blazing eyes directly at them and howled an unearthly howl up at the fog-shrouded full moon.

Then he half-walked, half-floated part way down the steep cliff wall. When the ranger shined his flashlight toward the dog, they saw that there was a small, hidden rock path leading up the face of the cliff. It had been hidden in the mist.

"Come on," said Rob, "Midnight's showing us the path!"

They scrambled up the steep rocky path. It was tough going, but they found that the dog waited for them. On and on the black dog led them, through thick bushes and under-brush, around wild rock formations, over giant boulders and thick tree roots. Every now and then, the full moon broke through the thick trees and lit up the ghostly forest scene. And always, the dog leading them on, waiting for them, his blazing red eyes leading the way.

After 45 minutes, when they were deep into the gorge, in an isolated place where none of them had ever been, Midnight stopped. He waited for them at the bottom of a tall, steep rock cliff. They could barely make out the top of the cliff. It had to be forty feet up.

Midnight stood on a small pile of rocks and dirt, which was overgrown with plants and bushes. In the light of the ranger's lantern shining through the fog, they watched as Midnight moved his head in that odd way again and again. He seemed to be directing them toward the mound of rocks.

"That's where he wants us to look," whispered Mike.

As if he had heard Mike's whisper, the great dog tilted back his head and howled at the full moon in a way that they had never heard a dog howl. The dog had in it fifty long years of sadness, heartbreak, and lonely wandering. It sounded human.

Then, as they watched, the dog seemed to slowly float up and away from them. The last thing they saw was the fiery red eyes floating away in the mist.

When the dog was gone, the ranger started to clear away the small pile of rocks and bushes where the dog had stood. Mike held the lantern.

After a few minutes of digging with his shovel, the ranger uncovered something small and white. He picked it up and held it in the lantern's light. It was a bone.

Working quickly, they soon found a small human skeleton, crumpled as if from a fall. The skull had a large crack in it. But touching the human skeleton was the skeleton of a huge dog. Around the dog's skeleton was a rotted leather collar that crumbled when Rob picked it up.

Attached to the collar was a dog tag. Rob held it with shaking hands. As they read the name in the light of the lantern, they heard in the distance the strange, unearthly howl of the ghostly dog who had led them to this spot.

The name on the dog tag was Midnight.

ABOUT THE AUTHOR

Katherine Burt lives in Columbus, Ohio. She makes her living as an editor.

She grew up in a small farming community in Lincoln County, Kentucky. In researching her father's family history, Katherine found many stories of ghosts, or "haints," as her family calls them. She also enjoys searching through old cabins near her parents' farm.

In Columbus, Katherine leads tours for children through the house of author James Thurber. So far, she has not seen the ghost who is thought to live in the house.